The Sugar Cup

READ ALL THE CANDY FAIRIES BOOKS!

Chocolate Dreams

Rainbow Swirl

Caramel Moon

Cool Mint

Magic Hearts

Gooey Goblins

The Sugar Ball

A Valentine's Surprise

Bubble Gum Rescue

Double Dip

Jelly Bean Jumble

The Chocolate Rose

A Royal Wedding

Marshmallow Mystery

Frozen Treats

COMING SOON:

Sweet Secrets

Candy Fairies

The Sugar Cup

HELEN PERELMAN

ILLUSTRATED BY
ERICA-JANE WATERS

ALADDIN
NEW YORK   LONDON   TORONTO   SYDNEY   NEW DELHI

ALADDIN

An imprint of Simon & Schuster Children's Publishing Division

1230 Avenue of the Americas, New York, NY 10020

First Aladdin paperback edition October 2014

Text copyright © 2014 by Helen Perelman

Illustrations copyright © 2014 by Erica-Jane Waters

Also available in an Aladdin hardcover edition.

All rights reserved, including the right of reproduction in whole or in part in any form.

ALADDIN is a trademark of Simon & Schuster, Inc., and related logo is a registered
trademark of Simon & Schuster, Inc.

For information about special discounts for bulk purchases, please contact
Simon & Schuster Special Sales at 1-866-506-1949 or business@simonandschuster.com.

The Simon & Schuster Speakers Bureau can bring authors to your live event.

For more information or to book an event contact the Simon & Schuster

Speakers Bureau at 1-866-248-3049 or visit our website at www.simonspeakers.com.

Book design by Karina Granda

The text of this book was set in Baskerville Book.

Manufactured in the United States of America 0814 OFF

2 4 6 8 10 9 7 5 3 1

Library of Congress Control Number 2014942340

ISBN 978-1-4814-0608-6 (hc)

ISBN 978-1-4814-0607-9 (pbk)

ISBN 978-1-4814-0609-3 (eBook)

For Teddy Hubbell,
a sugar-tastic *friend!*

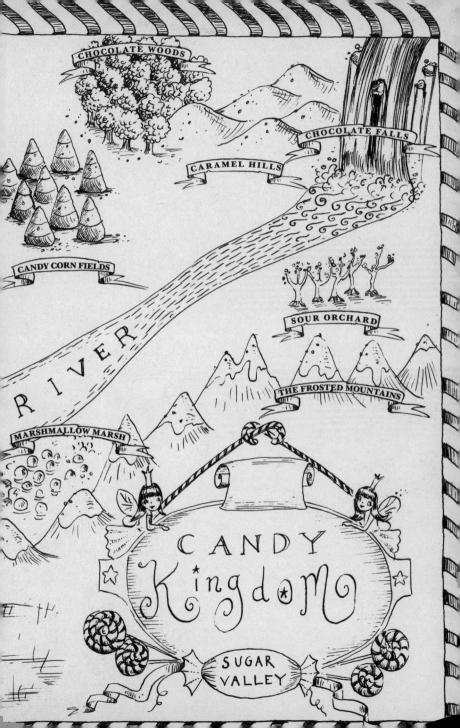

Contents

CHAPTER 1	Dipping Pair	1
CHAPTER 2	Minty Surprise	13
CHAPTER 3	Mint Mess	24
CHAPTER 4	Mint's Promise	34
CHAPTER 5	Feeling Sour	44
CHAPTER 6	Mint Masterpiece	54
CHAPTER 7	Sweet Apologies	66
CHAPTER 8	Delicious Music	75
CHAPTER 9	Frozen Mint	86
CHAPTER 10	Sweet Endings	96

Dipping Pair

Dash the Mint Fairy looked around Pepper-mint Grove. The bright morning light made her mint candy crop sparkle. Each mint was superwhite and just right for picking. She grabbed her harvest basket and started her work.

"Hi, Doopie," Dash said to the tiny chip-munk at her feet. She bent down and held out a mint for the small animal. "Here you go," she said. She watched the red-and-white-striped chipmunk hold the candy in her front paws and take a nibble. "What do you think?"

Doopie's happy squeak made Dash laugh.

"That is how I feel about a fresh mint candy too!" she said. "I'm glad that you agree."

Picking mints from the mint bushes wasn't an easy task. Dash had to reach in under branches to get the best ones. At times like these, she was happy to be a small Candy Fairy.

Dash held up one of the larger mints. She slipped it into her bag. Secretly, she had been painting mints with her new set of white-chocolate paints. She had just started doing this kind of artwork, and she loved it!

During the Sugar Cup Games, an event that

was happening in Candy Kingdom soon, decorating candy was one of the five events. The annual competition among fairies in Sugar Kingdom, Candy Kingdom, Cake Kingdom, and Ice Cream Isles was an exciting time. Cocoa, Dash's Chocolate Fairy friend, had competed in the Art Treat event last year. But this year Dash really wanted to enter.

When Dash had a full basket of mints, she headed to Chocolate River. She was meeting Cocoa for chocolate dipping. Nothing was more delicious than a mint freshly dipped in chocolate!

Dash was planning on talking to Cocoa about the Art Treat event. She just wasn't sure how to tell Cocoa. All her friends knew Dash loved to eat mints, but they didn't know how much she loved to decorate them! She loved the bold, bright colors swirling around and the messy, minty masterpieces she created.

"Hi Dash!" Cocoa called. The Chocolate Fairy was waiting at the shore of Chocolate River. She had two dipping rods with her. "I see you have lots of mints!"

Dash landed and put down her large basket. "Just picked! This is a good crop," she boasted. "I even got Doopie's approval."

"And such a big basket!" Cocoa exclaimed. "How did you fly with that?"

"I might be small, but I am strong," Dash said proudly. She held up her arms to show off her muscles. "Must be all those mighty mints I ate," she said, giggling. She looked out at the swirling river. "The chocolate looks *choc-o-rific*!" She rubbed her stomach. She settled down next to Cocoa. "This is a great day!"

Cocoa laughed. "I agree," she said. "But it would have been greater if we had received a sugar fly message from Candy Castle about the Sugar Cup Games."

"That's true," Dash said. "The games are in five days."

"We should hear today," Cocoa said. "This could be our year to win the cup!"

For the past four years, Cake Kingdom, which was ruled by Princess Lolli's sister, Princess Sprinkle, had been the winning kingdom. The kingdom that won brought home a golden trophy called the Sugar Cup. Princess Lolli's parents, King Crunch and Queen Sweetie, were the judges, along with other noble fairies. They would score the events and tally the scores.

Dash thought that now would be a good time to bring up the Art Treat. She looked over at Cocoa. "I saw Tula yesterday at Candy Castle," she said. She strung her mint on her dipping stick. Tula was one of Princess Lolli's trusted advisers and the one selecting fairies for the events. "She was asking me all kinds of questions about the Sugar Cup Games."

"I spoke to Tula too," Cocoa told her. "She said she was going to change things up this year."

"Huh," Dash said. She wanted to blurt out her wish to Cocoa, but she couldn't!

Cocoa strung a mint on her stick and dipped the candy in Chocolate River.

Dash fluttered her wings. Now would be a good time to tell Cocoa. "Do you think we'll be assigned different events from last year?" she asked. Her stomach did a tiny flip-flop.

"I'm sure you will be picked for racing," Cocoa told her. "Everyone knows you love racing the best."

"Hmm," Dash said, dipping her stick lower into the river. "What about you?" she asked. "You loved the Art Treat competition, right?"

"I did," Cocoa said, not looking at Dash.

Dash had a feeling that Cocoa wasn't telling her something.

Cocoa looked over at Dash. "Did you tell Tula what you want to do?"

Dash's face felt hot, like a cinnamon burst. "You know I love to race," she said quickly.

Oh no! Dash thought. *I had the chance to tell Cocoa and I didn't!*

Cocoa unhooked her dipped mint and dropped it into another basket. "That is what I thought," she said.

"Did you tell Tula you want to enter the Art Treat?" Dash asked. "I'm sure you already have so many ideas. You're the best artist."

Cocoa shrugged. "Thanks, Dash," she said.

At that moment Dash wished she hadn't told Tula about wanting to change events for the Sugar Cup. She didn't want to upset Cocoa.

The two friends sat on the riverbank in silence as they finished dipping the candy. Dash felt that Cocoa wanted to tell her something, and she wanted to ask Cocoa more questions, but when Melli the Caramel Fairy flew over, she lost her chance. Melli's wings were fluttering twice as fast as normal.

"Guess what? I am playing in the music competition and Berry is singing!" she exclaimed. "Raina has trivia again," she went on. "No one knows more about Sugar Valley history than Raina the Gummy Fairy! She will probably win first place again."

"Wow," Dash said. "Sounds like everyone got what they wanted."

Melli leaped up in the air. "And the best part is, the five of us were selected for the fast-fly relay race!"

"The fast-fly is really important and worth the most points," Dash said. "The five of us were picked for that?"

Melli reached down and took a chocolate-covered mint. "Yes," she said. "Can you believe it? We're old enough this year and we were picked!"

"Cool mint!" Dash exclaimed. "What about the other events?" she asked. She tried to act casual.

"I'm sure a sugar fly will find you before Sun Dip," Melli told them. "I'm off to see Berry so we can pick a song. This year we are going to try an even harder piece of music. Last year we weren't so good. But we've been practicing." She lifted off the ground. "Those chocolate mints are *sweet-tacular*! Bring them to Sun Dip! You two sure make a great pair."

Dash and Cocoa waved as Melli flew off.

Just then two sugar flies landed on the rim of

Dash's basket. Cocoa and Dash looked at each other and grabbed their notes.

When Dash saw her assignment, her wings tingled with delight. She *was* picked for the Art Treat! She looked over at Cocoa. Dash's wings drooped and she looked away. If Cocoa wasn't happy about her placement, Dash wasn't sure the Sugar Cup would be so sweet.

CHAPTER

2

Minty Surprise

Dash looked at Cocoa. She knew that she had to tell her friend about her event. She wasn't sure how Cocoa would react. Would she be mad? Was it possible she wasn't going to be in an event? Dash's head began to swirl. Finally she realized she had to just blurt out the fact . . . and get away fast! "I got picked for the Art Treat," she said very quickly.

Cocoa's eyes widened and her mouth opened. Dash grabbed her basket and shot up in the air.

"I'll see you at Sun Dip," Dash called from above. "Bye! See you later!"

In a flash, Dash was off. At times like these Dash was glad that she was a fast-flying fairy. She felt awful—and happy at the same time. She was secretly so excited about being chosen for art. She believed that she could do a great job decorating a plain candy. She did a few dips on the way back to Peppermint Grove.

As the sun got closer to the Frosted Mountains, Dash began to get that funny feeling in her stomach again. She knew she had to face Cocoa—and the other Candy Fairies. Would they all be mad at her too? Dash realized she had not even asked Cocoa what event she would be doing for the Sugar Cup. Now Dash felt even worse. Sometimes she was a bit too minty and rushed off without thinking. Maybe she would do something special at Sun Dip for Cocoa.

When Dash arrived at Red Licorice Lake for Sun Dip, Cocoa and Melli were already there. Seeing them together made Dash even more nervous. Maybe Cocoa was angry at her for taking her spot in the Art Treat and was talking to Melli about what to do. Dash was about to head in the other direction when she heard Melli call to her.

"Hey, Dash!" Melli called. "We were just talking about you."

Oh no! Dash thought. *Are they both mad at me?*

There was no escape! Dash had to face Cocoa. She glided down to the red sugar sand.

"You flew off so quickly earlier," Cocoa said as Dash landed. "Were you all right?"

Cocoa's concern for her made Dash feel rotten. She lowered her head. "Yes, I just felt funny receiving my Sugar Cup news with you," she said. She didn't dare look up.

"I'm sorry that I rushed off without asking about your event. Please don't be mad." She held her breath as Cocoa slowly responded.

"Well, I got . . . um . . ." Cocoa stumbled over her words. "I got racing," she finally said.

"Racing?" Dash said.

Cocoa leaped up in the air. "Don't be mad,

Dash," she said. "Maybe there was a mistake and our sugar flies got switched."

"I don't think so," Dash said. She felt her shoulders relax, and her wings fluttered. She smiled.

"Why are you smiling?" Cocoa asked. She gave Melli a worried look.

"Because I wanted art very much," Dash told her. "I spoke to Tula about switching events this year." She looked down at her dress. "I just didn't tell you."

Cocoa started laughing. "You mean we both got what we wanted? We both got what the other did last year?"

Dash scratched her head. "You wanted to race?" she asked. "This is a minty surprise!"

"Yes," Cocoa replied. "Ever since we competed together at Double Dip on Meringue Island, I thought it might be fun."

Double Dip was a race that Dash and Cocoa had been in together. The two-fairy sled race had been new for both of them. And lots of fun.

Melli took a deep breath. "Hot caramel!" she exclaimed.

"This is going to be the greatest Sugar Cup ever!" Dash cheered.

"It will!" Cocoa cried.

"What is all the celebrating for?" Raina asked. She landed next to Melli. "Did everyone hear about their Sugar Cup events?"

Melli fluttered her wings. "Yes, and it is unexpected," she explained. "Dash is going to do the Art Treat, and Cocoa is going to race!"

"Sweet sugars," Raina said. "That *is* unexpected." She looked at Dash and Cocoa. "But you both look superhappy."

"We are!" Dash and Cocoa said at the same time.

"It's almost time for Sun Dip," Raina said. "Where's Berry?"

"She's late, as usual," Melli said. "And I'll bet she is already figuring out what to wear for the music competition."

Berry arrived before her friends said anything else. "I chose that outfit a long time ago," she said, smiling. "A fairy should always be prepared with the perfect dress. Especially when performing!"

The Candy Fairies laughed.

"This is going to be the sweetest Sun Dip,"

Raina said. "We have lots to celebrate." She spread a blanket out on the sand.

"Especially with our freshly dipped candy," Cocoa said, pushing her basket to the middle of the blanket. "Dash and I dipped these mints in Chocolate River today. Aren't they *choc-o-rific?*"

"Sure as sugar," Melli said, popping a candy in her mouth.

"Cocoa, I can give you some great pointers on the race," Dash said. "You can use my sled, too."

"Thanks, but I'm borrowing a castle sled. Do you want to use any of my paintbrushes?" Cocoa replied. "And you can use my paints."

Dash saw a worried look on Melli's face. "What?" Dash asked her. "Why do you look so concerned?"

Melli shrugged. "Well," she said slowly, "I was just remembering the Double Dip race."

Dash turned a flying somersault. "You mean the race that Cocoa and I won?" she asked. She flew back down and hit a high five with Cocoa.

"Actually," Melli said, "I was remembering how hard it was for you two to practice and work together."

Dash rolled her eyes. "Oh, Melli," she said. "You worry too much. We'll be fine. Right, Cocoa?"

"Yes," Cocoa replied. "These practices will be much different. We won't be in the same sled!"

Berry decided to change the subject. "Look at the colors tonight," she said, pointing up to the sky. "There's nothing like the colors of Sun Dip."

As the sun slid behind the mountains and the deep purples and pinks of the sunset grew darker, the Candy Fairies watched silently.

Dash thought about what Melli had said. She looked over at Cocoa. Melli was always worried about something. Dash popped another mint into her mouth and gazed up at the pastel sky. Melli had nothing to worry about. She and Cocoa were perfect partners for candy, racing, and art. There was nothing minty about that!

CHAPTER

3

Mint Mess

The next morning, Dash went to Chocolate Woods. She was excited to visit Cocoa and get some helpful art tips from her. Now that she was chosen for the event . . . she wanted to win!

Cocoa greeted Dash at the door. "I have a surprise for you," she said, grinning. "I had

Berry make you a smock for painting." She held up the white apron for Dash.

"*So mint!*" Dash exclaimed. She slipped the apron on. "Now I feel like an artist!"

"Come out to my garden," Cocoa said. "This is where I love to paint. I especially like to paint my chocolate roses."

Dash followed Cocoa out to her rose garden. Cocoa was very proud of her chocolate flowers. She had set up two easels in the middle of the garden.

"Sweet mint!" Dash gasped. She saw a new brush on a tray with small circles of colors. "Is that mine?"

"Yes," Cocoa said, grinning. "This is an artist's palette." She opened a case of paints and squeezed out some colors onto another tray for herself.

Dash stared at the white canvas. Suddenly she was nervous. "I don't know what to paint!"

Cocoa sighed. "That is one of the hardest parts about being an artist," she said. "The first stroke!"

"I don't know," Dash said. She quickly started to splatter paint all over the canvas.

"Wait!" Cocoa cried. "What are you doing?"

"I am creating," Dash said, smiling.

"You are a creating a mess," Cocoa told her. "Slow down, Dash! This isn't a race. Art takes time and patience. You have to plan out what you are going to paint."

Dash eyed Cocoa. She had never thought of that. She never planned out her art. For her, the fun was mixing the bold, bright colors and splattering them. She took her brush off the canvas. "What do you mean?"

Cocoa showed Dash a piece of chocolate chalk that she used to sketch her ideas. "First I do the drawing lightly with a chalk," she told her. "This way, if I make a mistake, I can just swipe it away."

Watching Cocoa try to draw the perfect shape of a rose was getting boring, and Dash slumped down on the ground. She looked at her spattered canvas. She liked the way some of the colors blended into one another to create new colors. So what if she didn't have a plan? She was creating art . . . delicious art! Dash dipped her finger into the orange paint and tasted the sweet icing.

"Dash," Cocoa scolded, "if you eat the chocolate paints, you won't have enough to paint with!"

"Hmm," Dash said thoughtfully. "The colors are so delicious-looking!"

Cocoa leaned over to look at Dash's palette. "And you shouldn't mix all the colors together. You need to keep a neat work area."

"Says who?" Dash blurted out.

Cocoa put down her brush. "I'm just trying to be helpful," she said quietly. "You don't have to be so minty."

Dash touched up a few spots and mixed a few more colors. Probably no one would be able to tell what she was making, but she loved the colors and swirls that spread over the white canvas.

When she was done, Dash saw that Cocoa did not approve of her painting.

"Well," Cocoa said, "it is colorful."

Dash smiled. "Thank you," she said. She knew that Cocoa was searching for something nice to say. She looked up at the sky. The sun was right above them. It was almost noon and she still had chores to do in Peppermint Grove. "Well, I guess I'll see you later at fast-fly practice in Caramel Hills," she said. She flopped her brush down and leaped into the air. "I'll come back for my painting later. Thanks, Cocoa! You are supersweet."

Dash flew off and left Cocoa standing in the garden, staring after her. Dash figured that Cocoa was amazed at how fast she had finished her painting. She grinned. She was the fastest-flying fairy, and now perhaps the fastest painter!

Later that day, when Dash got to Caramel Hills for practice, Melli and Raina had already heard about her painting time with Cocoa.

"Dash," Melli said, "couldn't you have cleaned up your mess before you left Chocolate Woods?"

Dash's wings dropped to the ground. "Oh," she said softly. She realized that she had run off without helping to clean up.

"Cocoa was very bitter about the way you left her paints," Raina added.

Melli put her head in her hands. "I knew this was going to be a big mess. Why didn't you two just stick with what you know best for the Sugar Cup Games?"

Raina wrinkled her nose. "Well, that would

be boring," she said. "We are allowed to try new things!"

"Don't worry, I'll make it up to Cocoa," Dash told them.

"Fast-fly practice is not going to go well with the two of you sniping at each other," Melli added.

Dash waved her hand. "No, things will be fine," she said. "Mint's honor."

Raina and Melli raised their eyebrows and gave Dash a long look.

"Really," Dash said. "Trust me. I have a supermint idea that will make everything all right."

Dash hoped that her plan to win Cocoa over would work. With her giving Cocoa some tips on the slopes, there was no way Cocoa could lose.

"Cocoa is going to forget that she is angry with me," Dash told her friends. "Just watch and see!"

CHAPTER
4

Mint's Promise

Waiting for Cocoa to arrive at Caramel Hills was hard for Dash. Melli told her that Cocoa was with Berry, so Dash knew they'd be late. Dash circled around a large caramel tree. When she was nervous, she had to keep moving!

Melli was right—Dash *should* have cleaned up her painting mess at Cocoa's. She was just in such a rush to get back to Peppermint Grove! Knowing Cocoa, she had probably cleaned every strand of those brushes. Now Dash really had to make peace with her chocolate friend.

"I'll make it right with Cocoa," Dash told Raina and Melli. "I don't want her to be mad. She was really sweet to me. She tried to teach me about drawing and gave me those paints." She sighed. "Though we do have different styles."

"I can imagine," Raina said, laughing.

"I am sure Cocoa will be fine with an apology," Melli added.

"We all need to work together if we are going to win the fast-fly," Raina said.

Dash agreed. She continued circling the trees in Caramel Hills until she saw Cocoa and Berry.

"Cocoa," Dash said, flying up to greet her when she finally arrived. "I am really sorry about the mess I left. I should not have rushed off without helping you clean up."

Cocoa seemed happy at Dash's apology. "Thank you for saying that, Dash," she said. "I was surprised that you left so quickly."

"Well, I . . ." Dash struggled with her words. "I hope that you'll forgive me. It was really nice of you to offer the paints for practice." She tossed her head to the side. Then she added quickly, "I have a *sugar-tastic* idea! After fast-fly practice, we could go to Marshmallow Marsh and take a few sled runs. I'd like to give you some racing tips."

Dash saw Cocoa look over at Melli. Dash knew right away what the Chocolate Fairy was thinking.

"Please, Cocoa," she said. "It wouldn't be like those Double Dip practices. Mint's promise."

"We all know Dash is the fastest racer in Sugar Valley," Berry said. "Cocoa, you should listen to her."

Dash shot Berry a thankful look. She hoped Cocoa would change her mind. She held up her hands, pleading. "Mint's promise," Dash said. "I really do want to help."

Cocoa smiled. "Okay," she said. "After fast-fly practice, we'll take a run."

Dash leaped up and gave Cocoa a huge hug.

"Good. We'd better get started with practice now," Raina said. "First we need to decide the order of our relay team. Each of us needs to take one part of the flight."

"I should go last because I am the fastest,"

Dash boasted. Then she realized that she had spoken very loudly. She bit her lip. She didn't want to be too minty again. She looked at her friends. "If you think that is a good spot for me," she added quietly.

Cocoa rolled her eyes. "Of course," she said. "The last fairy should be the fastest."

"And a strong flier should go first so we get the lead," Raina said thoughtfully.

"Cocoa, you should take the lead," Dash said.

Cocoa seemed to like that idea, and the others agreed. Dash was proud of herself. She was keeping her mint promise. This wasn't so hard!

The practice went well. Each fairy had to fly one hundred yards. Raina's stopwatch clocked the fairies in at great times.

"We have a good chance this year," Raina said, looking over the times. "Those Cake Fairies will have some real competition this year."

"They haven't raced us before," Berry said. "They will be surprised!"

"It's a big deal that we are racing," Melli said. "The fast-fly counts double any of the other events."

"Which means we have an excellent chance of winning the cup!" Dash exclaimed.

As all the fairies were saying good-bye, Dash pulled on Cocoa's arm. "Are you ready to practice with me?"

"Yes," Cocoa said. "I bet we can get a run in before Sun Dip."

"Or two or three," Dash said eagerly. Then she noticed the look on Melli's face.

"Dash," Melli whispered, "remember you promised not to be so minty."

Dash nodded. "I know, I know. Mint's promise!"

Together, Dash and Cocoa flew to the slope on the Frosted Mountains where the Sugar Cup race would be held. Cocoa showed Dash her sled at the shed near the top of the mountain. Dash held true to her word and didn't say anything about Cocoa's sled. It wasn't a style that she liked to use for racing. The blades were a little too wide for her, but she didn't want to come across as too pushy. Instead, she showed Cocoa some cool ways to turn and slide. The practice was going well until the last run. Dash saw that Cocoa was holding her steering bar too tightly.

"You might want to ease up on your hold," Dash said. "If you hold too tight, you might throw off your balance."

Just as she said that, Cocoa fell off her sled and into a frosted mound. Poor Cocoa was covered in frosting! Dash couldn't help but laugh. She giggled and then tried to stop—which only made her giggle more.

Cocoa stomped her foot. "So much for 'mint's promise,'" she mumbled. She grabbed her sled and pulled it back to the shed.

Dash felt awful. "Oh, come on, Cocoa!" she begged. "It's funny. It's all in good fun."

"Not for me," Cocoa said. "Forget it, Dash. I don't need your help."

Cocoa flew off and left Dash alone on the slope. Dash lowered her wings and sighed. The

practice race hadn't gone as she'd planned—
and neither had her plan to make Cocoa feel
better.

Just then Dash saw a sugar fly. She decided
to send Cocoa a note. *Keep on track*, Dash wrote.
I believe in you! She thought
the note might make
Cocoa happy. At least,
she hoped it would
as she sent the
sugar fly off with
her message.

CHAPTER
5

Feeling Sour

Dash flew to Candy Castle early the next morning. She had an appointment with Tula. Tula was going to go over the rules of the Art Treat competition. Only now Dash was feeling unsure about her choice.

Maybe I can switch my event, Dash thought.

After yesterday's race with Cocoa, Dash had

started to miss racing. And all that talk of art technique with Cocoa had put her in a bad mood. Dash loved messy, fast art. Cocoa did not. Maybe the judges of the event wouldn't like Dash's art. Past winners of the Art Treat all had different styles. What would happen if the judges didn't like Dash's style? She didn't want to be the fairy who lost the Sugar Cup for Candy Kingdom because she had done so poorly at her event. And Cocoa hadn't replied to her sugar fly note. Maybe Cocoa was still upset with her. It was unlike her not to respond.

That did it. Dash made up her mind that she would ask Tula if she could switch her event. Dash flew around the gardens, looking for the wise fairy. The Royal Gardens were crowded with Castle Fairies setting up for the Sugar Cup Games. In three days the games would begin! Finally Dash found Tula.

"Sweet morning," Tula called to her. She flew over to Dash. "There's so much going on here today," she gushed. She looked down at her clipboard. "The slopes at the Frosted Mountains are set, and the stage for the trivia and music events is finished. We need to finish the Art Treat tent and mark the path for the fast-fly." She sighed. "So much to get done!" Tula looked up at Dash. "Why such a sad face?" she asked. "I heard you were excited about being picked for the Art Treat. You did request it, right, Dash?"

Dash fluttered her wings. "I was happy," she said. But she couldn't lie to Tula. "I think I miss racing more than I thought I would," she blurted out.

Tula was quiet for a moment. "I understand," she said. "You've always been our star racer. But isn't it nice to try something new?"

"Maybe," Dash said. "I was excited about the art, but, you see . . . Cocoa . . ." She couldn't finish her sentence.

Tula grabbed Dash's hand and brought her to a quiet spot in the garden. "New things are harder sometimes," she said. "And you and Cocoa are both trying new events. The good news is that maybe you can help each other."

"That would be good," Dash told her. "Only, we can't seem to help each other." She looked down at her feet. "We've been fighting."

Tula nodded. "Trying new things sometimes

makes you cranky, yes?" she said. "At least, that is how I feel. Oh, when I first had to fly up to Sugar Castle on a unicorn, I was crankier than an Ice Cream Fairy in warm weather." She smiled. "But now I don't know what I would do without these rides. And it's fun."

"Maybe switching was a bad idea," Dash mumbled.

Tula took off her glasses and let them hang down from the chain around her neck. "Dash, you were chosen for the Art Treat because you have a great chance of winning. Your work is exciting and bold," she told her. "And more important, you said you wanted to try this event. Remember?"

Dash thought back to

when she'd spoken to Tula about switching events. She had been so excited. That was probably how Cocoa had felt too.

"You and Cocoa are lucky," Tula went on. "This competition is supposed to be fun and give you a chance to do something you haven't tried before. Help each other!"

"We had a better chance when we were getting along," Dash mumbled.

"Oh, Dash," Tula sighed as she stood up. She put her glasses back on. "No more sad faces. Come, let me show you where the Art Treat is being held."

Dash followed Tula to another area of the Royal Gardens. She saw all the easels lined up where the fairies would be painting.

"Remember, Dash," Tula said. "This is not a

race. You don't have to finish in seconds. You will have about an hour to create your treat. The paints will all be here for you."

"So my fast art style is bad?" Dash asked. Her wings twitched. "That is what Cocoa told me."

Tula shook her head. "I know your work. You have your own style," she told her. "I'm just telling you that you don't need to rush."

"You don't think that I'm messy and sloppy?" Dash asked.

Tula smiled. "Not at all, Dash," she said. "You have a unique style, and if you take your time, I think you will create something original and delicious."

Dash blushed. "Thank you," she said. But she really didn't believe Tula. She remembered Cocoa's face when she had quickly splattered her paint. She was the only one who liked her art fast and messy! Dash wasn't sure what she should do.

"I have to fly," Tula told her. "Feel free to stay around and watch some of the other artists. You will see that everyone has a different style unique to them. Everyone brings something special to whatever they do—if everything looked the same, the world would be a very boring place."

Dash nodded.

"Everyone is flying in from the surrounding kingdoms today and tomorrow for the games," Tula continued. She pushed her glasses up on her nose. "I really have to fly. So much to do! Come by tomorrow and we'll talk more!"

"I'll see you later," Dash called out as Tula

flew off. She turned and looked around the gardens. Several fairies from different kingdoms were grouped together, laughing and getting ready for the competition. There were fairies practicing music, dance, and art. Dash remembered last year's Sugar Cup Games and how she'd had such a great time during the days before the race. She hadn't been nervous or unsure, and she'd had a great time visiting with old and new friends on the slope. This year everything was different. She felt out of place.

Looking around for a sugar fly, Dash felt hollow inside. Cocoa still hadn't responded to her note.

Dash left the Royal Gardens feeling sour about this year's competition and the choice she had made.

CHAPTER
6

Mint Masterpiece

On the way back to Peppermint Grove, Dash stopped off at Lollipop Landing. She found Melli and Berry practicing their song for the Sugar Cup Games. Dash landed quietly and listened. Melli was playing her licorice stick, and Berry was singing an old unicorn lullaby. They sounded *sugar-tastic*!

"Bravo!" Dash cried at the end. She leaped high up in the air to applaud her friends.

"Dash, I didn't see you," Melli said. "Did you hear the whole song?"

Dash clapped her hands. "Sure as sugar, you two will win the music competition," she said. "You have gotten so good."

Berry bowed. "Thank you," she said. "I think we've come a long way since last year's competition."

"Yes," Melli agreed. "We're doing a much harder arrangement this year," she added.

Dash was jealous. Maybe if she were racing, she could have done something extra-minty on the slopes. She could have wowed the judges. This year she could be the worst artist in the competition!

"Dash, how is your art coming along? And how is coaching Cocoa?" Melli asked. She put her licorice stick back in the case.

It was nice of Melli to ask, but Dash had a feeling that Melli had already heard all about the practice at the Frosted Mountains yesterday.

"Well," Dash said, "it probably wasn't the best practice run. I didn't mean to laugh when Cocoa tumbled and make her upset." She looked down at the ground. "She hasn't responded to my sugar fly note."

Berry looked over her shoulder. "Oh, that doesn't sound good," she said. "Is that why Cocoa couldn't stop to talk to me this morning? She was in a big rush to get to the slopes."

Dash dragged her foot on the ground. "I

wasn't so nice to Cocoa," she said. "I didn't mean to, but I laughed at her. She took a fast turn and wound up in the frosting." Dash sat down and grabbed a lollipop. "But to tell you the truth, I miss being good at something and having fun. Art is hard."

Melli sat down next to her. "Aren't you having fun with art?"

"Sometimes," Dash said. She was thinking about how she felt when she first started painting her mints. Painting bright, delicious colors on her white mints was fun. "I think Cocoa is more serious than I am."

"You can still be your fun, minty self," Berry said.

"Maybe," Dash said, thinking. "I'm jealous

that you both are doing something you know you are good at."

Berry put her arm around Dash. "Lighten up, Dash!" she said. "This is all supposed to be a good time. Just wait till those judges see your minty masterpiece."

Dash looked up at Berry. "Thanks," she said. "I hope you're right. I think I'm going to skip Sun Dip tonight," she added. She didn't feel like seeing Cocoa. "Please tell the others I was tired and I will catch up with them tomorrow."

Melli nodded. "We understand," she said. "Get a good night's rest. We'll see you at Candy Castle for the fast-fly trials tomorrow afternoon."

"I wouldn't miss it," Dash said. She was relieved her friends understood. Maybe tomorrow she would feel differently. Maybe after the practice Art Treat session in the morning and then the fast-fly relay she would be feeling better about the whole Sugar Cup Games.

At Candy Castle the next day, Dash saw Tula in the Royal Gardens again. Only this time, Tula was standing next to the Sugar Cup! Dash flew right up to the beautiful, shimmering gold sugar trophy. She couldn't take her eyes off the gorgeous prize. She had never seen the trophy so close up before.

"Look what arrived today from Cake Kingdom!" Tula exclaimed. "Isn't this exciting?"

Dash leaned in close to see the details on

the cup. "Oh, I hope this gets to stay here in Candy Kingdom," she said.

"We haven't had the Sugar Cup in Candy Castle for a few years," Tula said. "Maybe this is our time."

"It's been three years," Dash told her. "And I really, really hope we're the kingdom that wins and gets to keep the Sugar Cup this year."

Tula laughed. "Well, we have a supersweet chance," she said. "How are your art practices coming along?"

"I am trying out new ideas," Dash said. She kept her eyes on the cup. She wanted to reach out and touch it! The trophy was so shiny!

"Dash, I found some paintbrushes for you that I think you'll like," Tula said. "Stay here and I'll be right back."

"So mint!" Dash exclaimed. Maybe with the right brushes she would feel better about her artwork.

When Tula flew off, Dash looked around. No one was looking at the Sugar Cup—or her. She really wanted to touch the treasured trophy. Was it heavy or light? What would it feel like to hold the cup?

Dash flew up to the trophy and lifted it up off the pedestal. She held the Sugar Cup close. "Thank you for this award," she began. "It is a supersweet honor to win this for Candy Kingdom." She loved how the cup felt in her arms. She was feeling all puffed up and proud as she pretended to receive the Sugar Cup.

"Maybe you should be brushing up on your art skills and not accepting awards," Cocoa said as she suddenly flew overhead.

Dash quickly put the Sugar Cup down. "I was . . . I was just . . ." She didn't know what to say. She was embarrassed, and the look on Cocoa's face was making her very uncomfortable. "I couldn't help but hold it," Dash told her. "That was likely my only chance."

"Don't be silly, Dash," Princess Lolli said, surprising both fairies. She landed next to the Sugar Cup. "We have a good chance of winning this year. And I hear you and Cocoa are working hard on your events."

"Yes," Cocoa said. "I hope to do very well on the slopes." She gave Dash a cold, hard stare.

"Excellent," Princess Lolli said. "We are going to have an exciting competition this year against all the other kingdoms."

Cocoa's wings were twitching, and she quickly excused herself. "I have to meet a friend on the mountain," she said as she raced away.

Dash knew Cocoa didn't want to be around her. Her chilling stare and no response to her sugar fly note made Dash feel bitter about the Sugar Cup Games.

She didn't mention to Princess Lolli how she was feeling about her new event or that she and Cocoa were not getting along. She just smiled at Princess Lolli and then looked longingly at the Sugar Cup.

Just then Tula returned with Dash's new set

of brushes. She handed them to Dash. The brushes were gorgeous, and the gift made Dash brighten.

"*So mint!*" Dash exclaimed. "I feel like a real artist now," she said. The gift definitely lifted her spirits.

"Use them well," Princess Lolli said, smiling.

"Brushes don't make an artist," Tula told her. "*You* are the artist. Remember that, Dash."

Dash smiled as she held the wrapped set of brushes. Tula believed in her. Now more than ever, Dash wanted to win her Art Treat event . . . and the Sugar Cup!

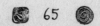

CHAPTER 7

Sweet Apologies

Dash set up an area in Peppermint Grove to practice her Art Treat designs. She lined up a couple of round, flat, fresh mints. The candies were just the right size for the contest, so she picked a few extra for her practice pieces. Dash mixed some colors and dipped her new brushes into the colorful icing. She splattered the paint and stood back to admire the design and colors.

"Hi, Dash," Cocoa said.

Above her, Dash saw Cocoa circling.

"Hello," Dash said. She wasn't up for another match of bitter words. She hoped that Cocoa wasn't still angry with her.

"I wanted to apologize," Cocoa said. She landed next to Dash. "I shouldn't have been so sour about your holding the Sugar Cup yesterday, and I should have sent you a sugar fly note back." She bowed her head and paused for a long time. "And I shouldn't have made such a big deal about your laughing when I got all that frosting on me." Cocoa looked up at Dash and smiled. "I have to admit, it was hilarious."

Dash giggled. She was glad that her old friend Cocoa was back. "I'm glad you are saying this," she said. She drew in a long breath. "And I'm really sorry too. I haven't been acting so sweet either."

The two fairies hugged.

"I like it much better when we aren't mad at each other," Dash said.

"Me too," Cocoa told her.

"When I was at Candy Castle yesterday," Dash said, "I saw lots of fairies having fun practicing for their Sugar Cup events. Remember when we used to feel that way about our events?"

"I know what you mean," Cocoa said. "Listening to Raina, Berry, and Melli the other day at Sun Dip, I was remembering how fun practices used to be." Cocoa looked Dash straight

in the eye. "You didn't come to Sun Dip . . . was that because of me?"

Dash didn't want to lie, but she was also done making Cocoa feel bad. "Let's not talk about that anymore," she said quickly. "Let's try to have a drop more fun." She held up a dripping brush. "I just mixed some new colors! Would you like to paint a little with me?"

Cocoa reached out for a brush. "Wow, these are beautiful," she said, admiring the new brush.

"Tula gave me a set of brand-new brushes," Dash told her. "And I am going to keep them as clean as you keep your set!"

Cocoa laughed. "Starting with clean brushes is important," she said. She looked over at Dash's mint. "I love how you drizzle the icing," Cocoa told her. "It's unique."

Dash stood up straighter. "Really? Wow, thanks, Cocoa. I've been trying to paint more like you. You work so neatly. The only thing is . . . I can't really do that."

Cocoa flapped her wings. "You shouldn't try to copy anyone," she said.

Dash blushed. "I know," she said.

The two fairies painted the mint candies together. Dash was so happy. It was like old sweet times, hanging out with her friend Cocoa. She started to hum as she painted. This was actually really fun!

"After we finish, do you want to come with me to the slopes? Maybe you could give me a couple more racing tips?" Cocoa asked.

Dash's eyes widened. "Are you sure you want me to come to the slopes with you?"

"Sure as sugar," Cocoa replied. "Your way of preparing for the race is different, but I would be foolish not to listen to a champion like you."

"Thank you," Dash said. "I was hoping you'd ask me. I'd love to race today. Let me just clean up here a little, and I'll meet you on the slopes."

Cocoa smiled. "Okay," she said. "I under-stand about that! I'd be happy to help you."

Dash took the brush from Cocoa. "No, you go and start practice," she said. "I owe you a cleanup!"

"Thanks, Dash," Cocoa said, grinning. "I'll see you at the finish line!"

When Dash reached the Frosted Mountains, she spotted Cocoa at the top of the slopes. She knew her friend had racing talent. Cocoa was fearless and knew when to lean in and when to hold back. She took her turns tight and fast. Cocoa was making great time on this run!

"You were *so mint* up there," Dash told Cocoa at the finish line. "I think that was your best time ever."

"I was thinking about what you told me the other day," Cocoa said. She took off her racing goggles.

"Really?" Dash asked. "I'm so glad that I was able to give you good advice!"

Cocoa grinned. "We do make good part-ners," she said. "Dipping candy, painting, rac-ing, and winning the Sugar Cup!"

"We hope," Dash added. She helped Cocoa pull her sled off the slope.

"I'm not sure that I'll be able to sleep tonight," Cocoa said.

"Me neither," Dash replied. "Tomorrow is the big event. Are you ready?"

"As ready as I'll ever be," Cocoa said.

Dash nodded. After all the practices, tomorrow was their one shot at winning the Sugar Cup for Candy Kingdom. But first she took one run down the slopes next to her friend.

8

Delicious Music

A loud, blaring trumpet sounded from Candy Castle. The Sugar Cup Games were about to begin! Dash flew over Sugar Valley, amazed at all the fairies flying toward Candy Castle. There were stages and banners set up all over the kingdom for the different events. The grandest events were the fast-fly and the closing ceremonies, but all Dash could think about was the Art Treat. She had to wait until the afternoon for her event. She didn't think she could wait that long!

The trumpets sounded again, and Dash swooped down to meet her friends at the entrance to the Royal Gardens.

"Can you believe all the fairies that are here?" Dash asked.

"This is the biggest turnout ever!" Raina exclaimed. "There are fairies from Cake Kingdom, Ice Cream Isles, and Sugar Kingdom, not only to compete but to watch!"

Cocoa took a deep breath. "And they all want to win the Sugar Cup," she said.

"But we're going to," Melli said, feeling proud.

Dash bit down on her lip. She was so ner-

vous! She never got this nervous before a racing competition! She looked down at the schedule Raina was holding. First there was the music event, then trivia, Art Treat, sled racing, and the fast-fly.

Berry flew down and put her hands on her hips. "Who's coming to hear Melli and me at the first event?" she sang out.

Everything about Berry was glittering and *sugar-tastic.* Her pink dress, her sugarcoated shoes, her perfectly braided hair . . .

Dash's mouth hung open as she stared at her friend. "Wow, Berry," she said. "You look scrumptious!"

Berry laughed. "I might have outdone myself with the sugar sparkles, but I wanted to make a statement," she said, smiling.

"Even Melli is wearing sugar sparkles," Raina said, admiring Melli's hair and outfit.

"Thank you for noticing," Melli said. She gently touched her new sparkling outfit. "This was all Berry's idea."

"I could have guessed that," Cocoa said, laughing.

Berry stood tall. "If you want to be a star,

you have to look like a star," she said.

Dash gazed at her two sparkling friends. They did look like shining stars. She was a little jealous, seeing how sure of themselves they were about their event. They were both so excited and didn't seem a drop nervous. Dash looked down at her own sweaty hands.

"And we're right behind you," Raina said, flying after them. "We want to get a good seat to watch!"

Dash, Cocoa, and Raina followed Berry and Melli to the corner of the Royal Gardens where a stage was set up for the music competition. There were many fairies in the audience from different kingdoms, waiting for their turn to show off their musical talents.

"Sweet caramel!" Melli exclaimed. "There

are Creamie and Dot!" She pointed to the Cake Fairies across the stage. "They won the duet last year." Melli blew a few notes into her licorice stick and looked around. "I don't remember there being so many fairies in last year's music event."

Berry put her hand on Melli's shoulder. "We sound great," she told her. "And we look great! This is going to be fun."

"You two are going to have the sweetest duet," Dash said. "A delicious unicorn lullaby. No one else is doing that!"

"Thanks, Dash," Melli said.

"Where are you going to sit?" Berry asked.

There were a few empty seats near the front of the stage. Dash slid down and put her hands on the bench. "We'll sit here," Dash told Berry and Melli. "We wouldn't miss watching and cheering you on!"

"Have fun!" Raina called.

"Sweet thoughts!" Cocoa cried.

"Thanks," Berry and Melli said as they flew off to take their places.

Princess Lolli took center stage and quieted the crowd. "Welcome to the Sugar Cup Games!" she said.

There was a huge roar of applause from the crowd.

"Thank you all for coming," Princess Lolli went on. "We're so excited about the Games this year. We wish you all good luck and a sweet time. Our first event is music. Please enjoy!"

The crowd cheered again and Dash held her ears. Would all these fairies be at her event too? Dash didn't want all these fairies watching her create her art. She didn't like when people stared at her. When she was racing, she was in her helmet and goggles and speeding down the slope, but there was no hiding or speed-ing away during the Art Treat. Her wings felt heavy and her stomach ached.

"Cheer up, Dash!" Raina said, giving her a poke. "We're just watching this event!"

"This is the easy part," Cocoa said, laughing.

Dash knew her friends were right. As the event started she tried to listen and enjoy the music. When Berry and Melli finished their piece, the crowd cheered loudly. But when the crowd roared this time, Dash didn't mind the loud noise. She was so proud of her friends!

Dash watched the judges talking and writing

down notes and scores. It was hard to wait for the final decision. She hoped her friends won!

Princess Lolli and her husband, Prince Scoop, got up and stood center stage. They gave the first-place medal to Berry and Melli. Her friends both had huge grins on their faces.

"Sweet sugars! We have a real chance of winning the Sugar Cup this year!" Raina cried.

"This was only the first event," Cocoa said. "Each of the events counts toward the final score. We all have to do well."

"But fast-fly is worth double," Raina added, grinning.

Dash started to feel the pressure.

"What if I totally blank out on the Art Treat?" Dash cried. She was nervous to face the blank candy. What if she couldn't paint what she had planned? Maybe she wouldn't be able to mix the right colors and the whole piece would turn a horrible color!

Raina put her arm around Dash. "Berry would say, 'Don't dip your wings in syrup yet.' The Sugar Cup Games are fun!"

"That's because Berry is wearing a first-place medal around her neck," Dash mumbled. She stared at Berry with her shiny, sparkling medal.

"Dash, stop worrying," Raina said.

Dash wanted to believe Raina. She took out her new brush set and held the brushes tightly in her hand. Maybe they would bring her the luck she needed.

CHAPTER

9

Frozen Mint

The hours leading up to Dash's event were as slow-moving as thick mint syrup. Dash couldn't enjoy the festivities around the kingdom at all. She could barely concentrate on Raina's trivia event. It was no surprise to anyone that Raina took first place.

Dash knew that Art Treat was next after the

trivia contest. She had a funny feeling from the tip of her wings to her toes. She couldn't move!

"Dash, you have to get to the art tent," Cocoa said. "Your event is about to start."

"Sweet strawberries," Berry said, looking at her. "I think Dash is frozen!"

Melli shook her head. "I've seen this before," she said. "Dash has stage fright!"

Cocoa put her hand on Dash's arm. "Dash, you are going to paint the best design," she said.

"I don't know," Dash said. She had trouble breathing and felt like her wings were made of lead. "I can't go!"

Dash felt her friends all staring at her. She wanted to show them that she could paint a mint, but she just couldn't.

"Oh, this isn't good," Melli muttered. "She's frozen mint!"

Cocoa stepped forward. "Listen, Dash," she said. "We know how you feel. You need to keep calm. Don't paint for everyone, just yourself."

"But everyone will be watching me," Dash said. She looked at all the fairies gathered near the art tent. It seemed that every fairy from every kingdom was curious about the Art Treat this year.

Finally Cocoa took Dash's hand in hers and flew her over to her painting area. There was a large white mint waiting for her with a new set of frosting paints.

"Why don't you lay out your brushes?" Cocoa asked.

Dash was so thankful for Cocoa. She listened

to Cocoa's voice and did as she said. She tried not to focus on all the other fairies. She looked down at her paints and set up her palette of colors. Cocoa stood off to the side with the other spectators.

"Welcome to the Art Treat!" Princess Lolli said to the fairies. "Fairies, take your brushes, and at the sound of the bell, we will begin!"

Dash heard the bell, but she didn't move. Once again she felt frozen like icing on the Frosted Mountains.

Then Dash looked over at Cocoa. Her friend smiled at her. Dash thought back to the day when they were dipping mints in Chocolate River and meeting their friends at Sun Dip that evening. The sky had been full of beautiful colors, and all her friends were together. She imagined sitting at Red Licorice Lake and watching the sun disappear as the pastel colors grew brighter across the sky. She took a deep breath.

Now Dash could see the colors in her mind. She opened her eyes and started to mix a few colors together. She didn't think about anyone else. Dash splattered and drizzled her paints. When she was done, the final bell rang out. She took a step back to admire her work. She had to smile. She had made her version of a Sun Dip scene.

"Dash, this is remarkable," Tula said from behind her. "You should feel very proud."

Dash stood up a little straighter.

"The piece is *choc-o-rific*!" Cocoa exclaimed.

"Oh, Dash!" Melli cried. "You did a *sugar-tastic* job."

"Sweet," Berry said, admiring Dash's work.

Raina gave Dash a hug. "I knew you'd do a great job."

Dash went over to Cocoa. "I was thinking about us the day we dipped mints, and that delicious Sun Dip," she told her. "Your smile when I was feeling stuck really helped me."

"Friends are for getting you unstuck!" Cocoa said with a smile.

"One hundred mint percent," Dash replied.

After a long wait, Princess Lolli came to the center of the tent. As the medals were given out Dash felt a little uncomfortable. Fairies from Ice Cream Isles, Sugar Kingdom, and Cake Kingdom took the top prizes. Dash didn't get a medal and was starting to feel extra-sad. And then there was an honorable mention for the most creative piece.

"Dash the Mint Fairy," Princess Lolli said loudly, "please come forward."

Dash raced to Princess Lolli. She bent her head down so Princess Lolli could place the fancy medal around her neck. Dash looked at the shiny medal and grinned.

"So mint!" she exclaimed.

Princess Lolli laughed. *"So mint,* indeed!" she proclaimed.

When Dash left the stage, she found Cocoa and gave her a warm hug. "Thank you," she said. "If it weren't for you, I would have been a frozen mint for the whole competition."

Cocoa laughed. "I'm glad that I could help.

You should be very proud. Especially since this was your first art competition ever."

"I am," Dash said. "And I owe it all to you." She gave her friend another hug. "Now it's your turn to sparkle!"

"I don't know about sparkling," Cocoa said. "I just want to cross the finish line in one piece!"

Cocoa left her friends and headed to the Frosted Mountains. Dash went to gather up her paints and brushes. She smiled again when she saw her finished work. The mint candy was not like anyone else's work. And she felt super minty proud.

"Dash, come quick!" Melli shouted.

Dash looked up and saw Melli flying toward her minty fast.

"Cocoa needs you!" Melli cried. "Please come quick!"

Dash wrapped her brushes and stuffed them into her bag. In a flash, she was off to the slopes. What could have happened to Cocoa? She hoped that nothing was wrong . . . but she had a bad feeling that this was not just a case of nerves.

10

Sweet Endings

When Dash arrived at the Frosted Mountains, a crowd had gathered along the racecourse. There was lots of excitement as the scoreboard counted down the minutes until the race began. Dash searched the starting line for Cocoa.

"Over here!" Cocoa called out to Dash.

Cocoa was sitting off to the side of the starting line. She was kneeling down next to her sled. "Dash, please help!" she cried.

Swooping down, Dash saw immediately why she had been called to the slopes. Cocoa's sled was missing a blade! There was no way she could race!

"What happened?" Dash asked, looking at the lopsided sled.

"The blade was wobbling and I tried to fix it," Cocoa said. She held up the blade. "I shouldn't have been playing around with the sled." She pulled off her goggles. "See, I shouldn't be racing!"

"Whoa! Hold on a minty minute," Dash

said. "This is not your fault. And we can fix this." She smiled up at Cocoa. "This happens all the time in racing."

Melli stood with Cocoa as Dash worked.

"What's going on?" Raina asked as she and Berry flew over.

Berry pointed up to the scoreboard. "You only have a few minutes until the start," she said.

"Hurry, Dash!" Melli said.

Dash stood up. She dusted off her hands. "It's all done," she said. She winked at Cocoa. "Nothing that I haven't seen before."

"Is the sled safe?" Melli asked.

"Sure as sugar," Dash said. "Sometimes the blades get jammed and I have to tighten up the screw. The sled is better than ever!"

"Thank you, Dash," Cocoa said.

"Remember, that is what friends are for . . . getting you unstuck!" Dash exclaimed.

Cocoa put her racing goggles back on and picked up the rope to drag her sled to the starting line. "Sure as sugar!" she cried. "Wish me luck!"

"You don't need luck," Dash said, smiling. "You have skill."

"Thank you," Cocoa said.

"I know the perfect spot to watch the race from. It's near the finish line," Dash told her friends. She led them to a tree with a long branch. The four friends sat in a row on the branch.

"Go, Cocoa!" Dash cheered.

When the blast sounded to start the race, Dash couldn't sit still. She knew many of the racers and enjoyed seeing them all zoom down the slope. Dash was the loudest fairy in the crowd. Cheering Cocoa on was supersweet.

"Peppa and Menta are superfast," Raina said, looking though Berry's candy-sparkled binoculars.

"They always are," Dash said, sighing. The two sisters were not always so nice, and they were usually Dash's biggest competition whenever she raced. "Look how close Cocoa is to Menta's sled. Maybe she'll catch up on the last turn."

"I hope so," Melli said, holding her hands tightly under her chin. "I can't stand to watch!"

"But Cocoa is doing so well!" Dash said, beaming with pride. "She's doing all the tricks that I told her to do out on those turns. She has a chance."

"Come on, Cocoa!" Berry cheered.

"You can do it!" Raina yelled.

Dash watched closely as the racers headed into the last turn. She wished with all her heart that Cocoa's sled would speed away and fly in first.

Instead, Menta took the lead. And her sister followed.

Cocoa came in third.

Dash and her friends flew over to Cocoa. There was a crowd at the finish line.

"I'm sorry I didn't win," Cocoa said. "I did my very best, but those other fairies were superspeedy."

"Don't be sorry!" Dash said. "You were *so mint*!"

Cocoa smiled. "Thanks, Dash."

"You were a pro," Melli added.

"Come on," Raina said. "We have to get back to Candy Castle for fast-fly."

"Let's go!" Berry said.

Raina clapped her hands. "I have been adding up our scores. If we win first place in fast-fly, we could win the cup!" she said.

"Really?" Melli cried. "Oh, sweet sugar! So much pressure!"

"We can do this!" Berry exclaimed. "Our practice times have been sweet. We've got this race."

"Just fly like we've done in practice," Raina told her friends. "We've been having great times. Berry's right, we have this!"

"But we weren't racing anyone in practice," Cocoa said.

"So we'll fly even faster!" Dash chimed in. She fluttered her wings. "I'm ready to fly. Who's with me?"

The five Candy Fairies all put their hands into the middle of their circle and did a team cheer.

"That's my team," Princess Lolli said. She flew over to her fairies. "Go fly," she said. "And have fun!"

"We will!" Dash cried as they sped off to Candy Castle.

Dash's hands started to sweat as she got into her position. There were fairies from each kingdom at each position. Dash couldn't see Cocoa, but she heard the trumpet blare to announce the start of the race and heard the crowd roar. Squinting, Dash could see Melli waiting for the baton to get to her.

Melli was up against one of the strongest fliers in Cake Kingdom. The Cake Fairy's wings were double the size of Melli's wings! Dash was getting nervous. Raina was next, and Dash knew that Raina had the power to take on the smaller Ice Cream Fairy. When Melli reached Raina, Raina reached out and took the baton. She sped toward Berry.

"Way to fly, Raina!" Dash cheered. She started fluttering her wings, waiting for her turn. She couldn't wait to get the baton. Berry made superfast time and handed off the striped mint baton to Dash.

"Bring it home!" Berry shouted.

And Dash was off. She flew as fast as she

could. She couldn't hear the cheers or see the other fairies along the sidelines. She had her eye on the finish line. And the Sugar Cup!

Dash made it across the finish line—and she was first! In a flash, her friends were all around her.

"The Candy Fairies win!" a voice boomed.

"We did it!" Cocoa shouted. She grabbed Dash and gave her a tight squeeze.

"Sweet sugar!" Melli said, smiling.

The five friends huddled in a circle.

Princess Lolli came over to the winning team. "I am so proud of you," she said. "That was great teamwork."

"But was it enough to win the Sugar Cup?" Dash asked.

"Yes," Tula said, grinning. She came up next

to Princess Lolli. "Candy Kingdom won!"

Dash's mouth fell open. "You mean we really won the Sugar Cup?"

"Yes," Princess Lolli said. "You all worked very hard. I am so proud of this team. The closing ceremonies and the presentation of the Sugar Cup trophy will be starting soon. Let's get back to the Royal Gardens."

All the fairies from all the different kingdoms gathered in the Royal Gardens. Again the trumpets blared. There was a long parade of all the fairies involved in the games. Once everyone was seated, Princess Lolli began the presentation.

"I am very proud to announce that this year's Sugar Cup goes to Candy Kingdom," she said. "Congratulations!"

The five Candy Fairy friends flew to the stage.

Princess Lolli handed the golden cup to Dash and Cocoa.

"Now you can say your speech for real," Cocoa whispered to Dash.

Dash grinned. "The Sugar Cup is beautiful and, winning is *sweet-tacular*," she said to the cheering crowd. "And it is especially sweet when the prize is shared with good friends."

"This is the sweetest ending to a Sugar Cup Games ever!" Cocoa added.

Dash passed the trophy to each of her teammates. Never had winning a trophy been so special and sweet.

Sparkle Spa

A BRAND-NEW SERIES FROM ALADDIN!

Making friends one Sparkly nail at a time!

All That Glitters

Purple Nails and Puppy Tails

Makeover Magic

True Colors

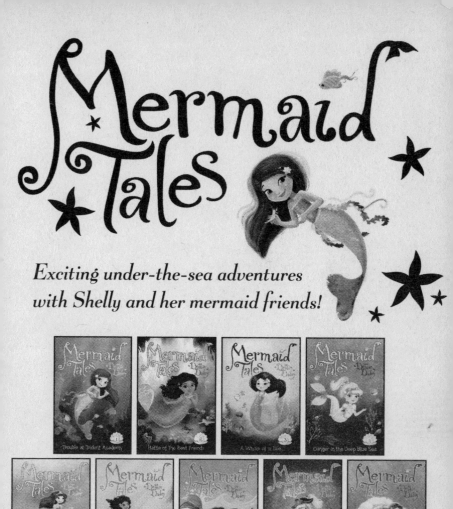

Goddess Girls

READ ABOUT ALL
YOUR FAVORITE GODDESSES!

#15 APHRODITE
THE FAIR

#14 IRIS
THE COLORFUL

#13 ATHENA
THE PROUD

#12 CASSANDRA
THE LUCKY

#11 PERSEPHONE
THE DARING

#10 PHEME
THE GOSSIP

#9 PANDORA
THE CURIOUS

#8 MEDUSA
THE MEAN

#1 ATHENA THE BRAIN

#2 PERSEPHONE
THE PHONY

#3 APHRODITE
THE BEAUTY

#4 ARTEMIS THE BRAVE

#5 ATHENA THE WISE

#6 APHRODITE
THE DIVA

#7 ARTEMIS THE LOYAL

THE GIRL GAMES:
SUPER SPECIAL

EBOOK EDITIONS ALSO AVAILABLE

Nancy Drew and The Clue Crew®
Test your detective skills with more Clue Crew cases!

#1 Sleepover Sleuths
#2 Scream for Ice Cream
#3 Pony Problems
#4 The Cinderella Ballet Mystery
#5 Case of the Sneaky Snowman
#6 The Fashion Disaster
#7 The Circus Scare
#8 Lights, Camera . . . Cats!
#9 The Halloween Hoax
#10 Ticket Trouble
#11 Ski School Sneak
#12 Valentine's Day Secret
#13 Chick-napped!

#14 The Zoo Crew
#15 Mall Madness
#16 Thanksgiving Thief
#17 Wedding Day Disaster
#18 Earth Day Escapade
#19 April Fool's Day
#20 Treasure Trouble
#21 Double Take
#22 Unicorn Uproar
#23 Babysitting Bandit
#24 Princess Mix-up Mystery
#25 Buggy Breakout
#26 Camp Creepy

#27 Cat Burglar Caper
#28 Time Thief
#29 Designed for Disaster
#30 Dance Off
#31 The Make-a-Pet Mystery
#32 Cape Mermaid Mystery
#33 The Pumpkin Patch Puzzle
#34 Cupcake Chaos
#35 Cooking Camp Disaster
#36 The Secret of the Scarecrow
#37 The Flower Show Fiasco

FROM ALADDIN • PUBLISHED BY SIMON & SCHUSTER